Copyright © 2005 by Magic Wanda Media (a division of Gobsmack Productions Limited)
Published by Magic Wanda Media (a division of Gobsmack Productions Limited)

Written by Renée Edwards
Illustrated by Bob Gauld-Galliers
Designed by Jag Matharu
Story Consultant: Barbara Chinn
Poem written by Barbara Chinn
Cover photography by Malcolm Tute
Edited by Jacqueline Fortey
Activity designed by Wendy Swan

First edition published 2005
Printed and bound by Thomson Press
www.MagicWandaMedia.com
ISBN 0-9548715-1-0

10 9 8 7 6 5 4 3 2 1

A CIP catalogue record for this book is available from the British Library.

MAGIC WANDA

Wanda
the Dragon

Cloaked by fluffy white clouds up in the sky,
The Island of Nimbi slowly floats by.
It's home to Wanda, Baz and Nubinu,
Richie, Mix-it-well, Mo and Doowott too!

Whilst moonbeams play and you're sleeping at night,
Mix-it-well rides on his Stirring-wheel bike.
He pedals away making magic steam,
Which drifts down to earth to bring you your dreams.

When morning comes to chase the night away,
You wake up and get ready for your day.
If you forget everything you've dreamed about,
From Volcano Mo your dream stuff pops out!

PLOP! Onto the Dream Dump your dreams then fall,
And Doowott turns up to tidy them all!
He never knows what magic he will find,
Lost and forgotten by your sleepy mind.

Doowott
the Dragonflyer

Baz Nubinu Spotted
Richie

Dream Dump

Nimbi Island

Volcano Mo

Now, Wanda the Dragon loves finding out
The secrets of things you have dreamed about.
Along with her friends, she will choose each day
A dream before it is tidied away.

The dragons then take the object they've found,
And fly through the Dream Steam, down to the ground.
They find the dreamer and give back the dream,
To discover what this special dream means.

Once they have found out all there is to know,
Through the Rainbow Gate to Nimbi they go.
They share with Mix-it-well what they have learned
About the special object they've returned.

Who knows, one day perhaps Wanda will bring
a dream back to yoooooooooou!

Everard
Mix-it-well

_____

I am the owner of this book

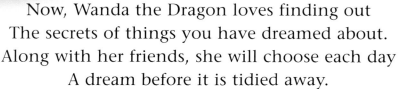
Dream-finder

For Max, Olivia, Anaïs and Rose

MAGIC WANDA
AND THE GARDENER

written by
Renée Edwards

illustrated by
Bob Gauld-Galliers

Magic Wanda Media, London

Early one morning, the young dragons were playing happily in the Dream Dump. Wanda and Nubinu were making a daisy chain for the old dragon, Everard Mix-it-well. It was his birthday.

"How old is Mix-it-well?" asked Richie,
who was dangling upside down like a bat
and flapping his one wing.

"He's very, very old," shouted Baz, as he climbed to the top of the Dream Sculpture. "I think he's one hundred years old today!"

"Let's make the daisy chain with one hundred daisies!" said Wanda.

"Dream on," said Nubinu. "How can we find one hundred daisies?"

"Do you think it takes one hundred days to grow one hundred daisies?" asked Richie.

None of the dragons knew the answers.

In his cave inside Mo the Volcano,
Mix-it-well, the old Dream-maker, smiled.
Last night he had enjoyed a birthday dream.

Far below in People Land, Lily the Gardener was dreaming about some magic seeds and a watering can.

Then Lily's dog came to wake her up.

"Good morning, Lemonhead," she said, and forgot all about her dream.

High in the sky on Nimbi Island, as Wanda and Nubinu finished making the daisy chain, something popped out of the yawning mouth of Mo the Volcano. It was Lily's forgotten dream.

The dream object landed next to Baz.

"Wow, Dream Power!" said Baz, "I wonder what this is."

He tipped up the dream object. Water rained out of the spout onto the three little dragons below.

"It's a rainmaker!" cried Baz.

Wanda thought it was raining and jumped up to look for a rainbow.

"Yippee, puddles!" said Richie, spinning down to the ground.

A rainbow laughed in the sprinkle.

They all chased after Baz. Round and round the Dream Sculpture they ran. Then they zigzagged back and forth all the way to Mix-it-well's cave, with water spraying from the spout of the dream thing as they went.

Suddenly, Richie spun round into a giant jelly that Doowott was struggling to pull along.

"Oops-a-daisy!" said Nubinu.

"Oops-a-jelly!" buzzed Doowott. "Why, oh why, would someone dream about jelly and cakes? I really don't know what to do with it all."

"Perhaps we can have a birthday party for Mix-it-well," said Baz, "and we can eat up all the party food."

Doowott beamed. "Yes," he said, "what a great idea! Let's go and find Mix-it-well!"

They found Mix-it-well paddling in a puddle.

"Happy Birthday!" they shouted,
  as Nubinu gave him the daisy chain.

Baz handed him the object.

"Is this dream object with a spout
  What all this water is about?"
  asked Mix-it-well.

"Yes," said Baz, "I think it's a rainmaker."

"And he's rained all over me,"
  grumbled Nubinu, who was soaking wet.

Mix-it-well nodded wisely and said:

"When we're asleep, we often dream,
Yet things may not be as they seem.
Go and meet this special dreamer,
Ask about the water streamer,
And as its story is retold,
Its uses or meaning will unfold."

He placed the magic Dream-finder
around Wanda's neck.

"Use the Dream-finder to find your way
And return home by playtime today."

The dragons were about to set off, when
Richie remembered the jelly and cake.

"Would you like to have a birthday party
at playtime?" he asked Mix-it-well.

Mix-it-well answered:

"Mmm yes, yes, I think I would,
  Birthday parties are so good.
  It's true I've seen one hundred years,
  Yet, at parties age disappears."

Then off flew the young dragons to People Land.

The Dream-finder led them through the Dream Steam, to a little street, in a little town, on a little island, with little hills. In the street was a little…

...shop.

The shop sold flowers
and plants, and outside
stood a big horse called 'H'.

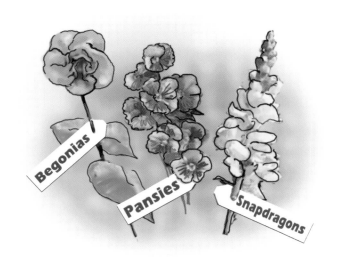

H had a cart that was overflowing with flowers.
There were beautiful orange Jamboree begonias,
blue pansies and yellow snapdragons. It smelt
wonderful to everyone except Baz.

"Pooh, this stinks!" said Baz, and sneezed.

"It grows on you," said H the horse.

"Are you a dragon?" asked Richie.

"No, I'm a horse!" said H. "Dragons aren't real!"

The dragons laughed and rolled
around – that was the funniest
thing they had ever heard.

"Dragons!" said Lily, coming out of the shop.

"We come from Nimbi Island in the sky,"
said Wanda. "That's where dreams are made
and where they return when you forget them."

"We've brought your dream back," said Baz.

"It's true! Last night I did dream about this watering can and some magic seeds," said Lily.

"What's a watering can?" asked Baz.

"Come on," said Lily. "I'll show you."

The dragons followed her into the shop
and out through an archway of sweet
peas and runner beans and into…

...Lily's beautiful garden.

It was full of all kinds of everything that can be grown from a seed, or a pip, or a stone, or a bulb. Birds sang as they fluttered in the branches of an apple tree. Butterflies flitted amongst the currant bushes and busy bumblebees buzzed around the flowers, collecting nectar to make honey.

"Wow!" said the dragons, looking at the fruit trees and the tree house where Lily lived.

"I'm a gardener," said Lily. "I use the watering can to water my plants."

Soon the dragons were busy helping Lily in the garden.

Richie sowed rows of lettuce seeds and Nubinu pulled up some carrots. Baz watered forget-me-nots and roses with the watering can, and Wanda filled a wheelbarrow with cornflowers and yellow lilies.

"You are very helpful dragons," said Lily. "I'd love some helpers for something special today. H and I are taking flowers to the school where the children are making a float for the flower festival. Would you like to stay for the parade?"

"Oooh, yes please!" cried the dragons, who didn't really know what a float was and were eager to find out.

H the horse plodded slowly up to the school and stopped. The children were making a big blue rabbit with a huge orange carrot in its mouth. Lily's flowers were just what they wanted.

Lily and the dragons helped the children create the float. They covered the shapes with flowers until the float was finished.

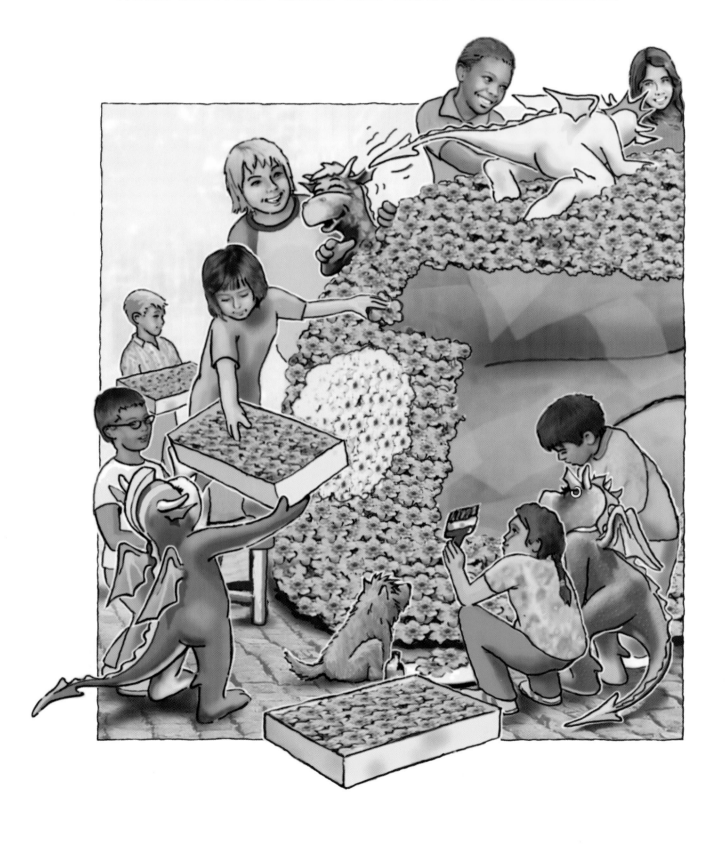

Then their beautiful float joined the parade,
moving slowly through the town. Everyone
had a great time. The day was even more special
because Wanda and her friends were there too.

After the parade they went back to the garden
to make Mix-it-well a fresh, flowery, fruity gift.

Wanda and Baz
climbed a tree to
pick apples, Nubinu
gathered some flowers
and a prickly cactus,
and Richie picked
some grapes.
Lemonhead found a
stick because that was
a doggy thing to do.

"Lily, does it take one hundred days to grow one hundred daisies?" asked Richie.

"Not so long," Lily replied. "You can plant one hundred seeds all at once and watch them grow together. Do you know what all flowers love?"

"I do!" neighed H, looking self-important and swishing his tail!

"Perfume?" asked Baz.

"It's water," said Lily. "All plants love water!"

H looked surprised.

Lily continued, "Water, earth, sunshine and a little magic."

"And a little manure!" thought H.

Soon it was time for Wanda
and her friends to go home.

"Goodbye!" said the dragons.

"Come and see us again," called Lily.

"There's always something new to
learn around here," neighed H.

Up, up flew the dragons, through
the Rainbow Gate to Nimbi Island.

When they landed in the Dream Dump,
they were amazed. There were carpets of
daisies and blue forget-me-nots everywhere.
Wherever they had raced that morning,
the magic seeds from Lily's dream
had fallen, grown and blossomed.

Mix-it-well and Doowott
were waiting for them.
Baz gave Mix-it-well the present.
The old dragon WAS pleased.

The dragons told Mix-it-well and Doowott
all about their adventures in People Land.
Mix-it-well took a bite from an apple,
looked thoughtful and said:

"This tale of gardening brings the splendid news
 That we can grow whatever we choose!
 Why, it's completely within our power
 To enjoy a constant flower shower!
 This apple's yummy and now we know
 If we plant its pips they will grow!"

Then Wanda made up a special birthday
song for Mix-it-well, and everyone joined in:

"Mix-it-well, we'd like to say,
Happy Birthday for today
And may all your dreams come true!
Mix-it-well we all love you!"

Mix-it-well replied:
"Now come along, let's celebrate,
My birthday party just can't wait!"

And what a party it was!

The old dragon had a very, very,
very happy 100th birthday.

Whilst they ate, a large animal-shaped
dream thing popped out of the mouth
of Mo the Volcano, as she hummed
the birthday tune.

Dream-time had begun
once more.

GROW YOUR OWN DREAMSTALK

What do I need?

- A runner bean
- Jam jar (clean and dry)
- Old magazines or catalogues
- 'Rainbow' – thin garden sticks, pipe-cleaners, coloured straws, bamboo cane or a long, smooth twig
- Paint (e.g. poster paint)
- Glue (e.g. white water soluble)
- Crayons, coloured pencils, or felt tips
- Scissors
- Small jug of water
- Paintbrushes
- Tracing paper
- Blotting paper
- Rubber bands
- Thin card
- Sticky tape

How do I make it?

1. To make a landscape for People Land, choose some pictures, from magazines or catalogues, of houses, cars, flowers, whatever you like, together with some of your own drawings. Cut them out and glue them around the outside of the jam jar.

2. Cut a piece of blotting paper to fit around the outside of the jar. Then roll it into a cylinder shape and use to line the inside wall of the jar.

3. Pop the bean in between the blotting paper and the wall of the jar, and push it down until it is where you would like it to be in your landscape.

4. Carefully pour some water onto the blotting paper that is lining the jar, until it is completely damp. Make sure there's at least 1 cm of water in the bottom of the jar.

5. To make the rainbow, paint seven garden sticks or use coloured pipe-cleaners, one in each of the following colours: red, orange, yellow, green, blue, indigo and violet. Then bind them together at the bottom and top with rubber bands.

   Or, you can paint a nice fat twig or piece of bamboo cane in rainbow stripes. Or just use a bundle of brightly coloured straws tied together with rubber bands!

6. Stand the rainbow in the jar. If you have used pipe-cleaners, you can bend them into a curve.

7. Draw a picture of Nimbi Island on the thin card, colour it in and cut it out. Or you can trace the one on the next page.

8. Fix Nimbi Island to the top of the rainbow with sticky tape.

9. In about a week your bean should start to sprout. Remember to keep the water topped up. As the Dreamstalk grows, wind it round the rainbow so that it grows towards Nimbi.

Bean

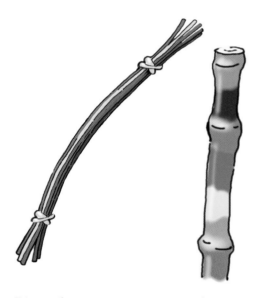

Pipe-cleaners   Bamboo cane

Tracing Nimbi Island

How to trace Wanda and Nimbi Island

Place the tracing paper over the image and carefully go over the outline with a pencil. Turn the tracing paper over and scribble over the outline. Turn the tracing paper the right way up, place it on the thin card and go over the outline again. Then colour your picture in and cut it out.

FOR ADULT HELPERS

What will children learn?
Watching the bean sprouting roots and shoots is a lovely way for children to learn how seeds germinate. This activity can be used to stimulate discussion about what a seed needs to start and to continue growing, covering topics such as water, light, change and the passage of time. Encourage children to keep a record of the developments they see. The activity also includes a number of skills to help develop hand-eye coordination such as colouring, gluing, tracing, sticking, and cutting.

Another fun idea
To add an extra feature, Wanda can be drawn or traced onto card and attached to the rainbow. Then she's ready to be moved gently up the rainbow towards Nimbi, as her Dreamstalk grows! When the Dreamstalk gets too big for the jar, you can plant it out in a pot or in the garden.

Acknowledgements

Renée thanks everyone who has contributed to this series with special thanks to her family, Gill Baxter, Gavin Bell, Lizzie Brown and family, Belinda Blanchard, Lily and Tim Bryant, Barbara Chinn, Cheryl Cohen, Celeste and Joe Collier, Nic Crampton, Lucy Darwin, Derek Dearden, Dora Dewsberry, Richard Dove, Brandi Edwards, Linda Edwards, Jacqueline Fortey, Katherine Gang, Debbie Gray, Rioja and Hamish Gwynne-Porter, Chris Legee, Kim Lombard, Dominique Naddeo, Kathleen Neale, Bonnie Poole, Claire Reynolds, Tiffany Sturge, Wendy Swan, Mary Taylor, Tam Ying Wah, Jane Wilford.

DVD credits

Presented by Magic Wanda Media
Executive Producer: Renée Edwards
Produced by Wendy Swan
Written and directed by Renée Edwards
Narrated by Fenella Fielding
Gardening by Nikki Mager
Production Manager: Claire Reynolds
Starring Claire, Jim, Jamie, Iestyn and Tizzie Harris and Celeste Collier

Director of photography: Colin Butler
Sound recording by Cormac Tohill
Second camera and additional sound by Robert Wilkins

Dream-finder prop by Mark Wheeler
Gardening props by Barbara Chinn
Animation by The Icing
Music production by Kim Lombard and Andrew Belling

Audio post production by Andrew Sears
Voice-over recording by Phitz Hearne
Online editing by Richard Cradick
Voice casting by Mandy Steele
Costumes by Katie Chebatoris
Photography by Malcolm Tute

Rostrum by King Camera
DVD authored by The Pavement
DVD face by Jag Matharu
Web design by Instinct Media
Website: www.MagicWandaMedia.com

With thanks to: Columbia Road Flower Market; George Gladwell; The Royal Botanic Gardens, Kew; Tower Hamlets Film Office

Magic Wanda and the Gardener
Listen to Fenella Fielding narrate the story (17 mins)
Read along with Fenella Fielding (18 mins)

Ruby and the Secret Dragon Garden
Watch Ruby discover gardening (11 mins)

Making a Secret Dragon Garden
Learn how to make a Secret Dragon Garden
with Nikki Mager (4 mins)

Magic Wanda Karaoke
Wanda Sing-Alongs (1 min 25 secs)